For all my godchildren,
who keep me young at Christmas!

BOOKS

Published by

Corner To Learn Limited
Willow Cottage • 26 Purton Stoke
Swindon • Wiltshire SN5 4JF • UK

ISBN 978-1-905434-14-5

First published in the UK 2007
Text © Neil Griffiths 2007
Illustrations © Gabriella Buckingham 2007

Design by David Rose
Printed by Tien Wah Press Pte. Ltd., Singapore

Sam's Sack from Santa

Neil Griffiths

Illustrated by
Gabriella Buckingham

It was almost silent outside as Sam lay still beneath his soft bed covers.

This year, as every year on Christmas Eve, he peeped out towards his bedroom window hoping to see or hear the slightest sound of Santa's arrival.

One year he thought he'd heard reindeer's feet thudding on the roof, but it was only his Dad thumping up their wooden stairs.

On another, he thought he'd heard Santa's bells, but it was his Dad again, putting out the milk bottles!

But tonight, all was very quiet and still.
The sky was amazingly clear, full of
winking stars and a glowing moon.
"Perfect for Santa-spotting," he thought.
   So Sam waited and watched ... Waited
and watched.

He began to wonder if
Santa had received his
letter asking for a kite.

Then he began to worry if Santa could squeeze down the narrow chimney and would he find the mince pie, sherry and carrots he had left for him and his reindeer?

Suddenly, the silence was broken by a large thud! Was it Dad again? No, it couldn't be, he could hear him snoring down the hallway. It **must** be Santa! Sam crept to the bedroom window and peered towards the garden below. There, right in the middle of the frost-covered lawn, was a large sack!

"Oh, no," thought Sam,
"he's missed my chimney!"
Sam put on his slippers and
tiptoed downstairs and
out into the garden.

He looked everywhere in the
hope of seeing Santa and his
sleigh, but he was nowhere
to be seen. Just winking
stars and a glowing moon.

Sam's disappointment soon disappeared when he saw his sack bulging with presents. He decided to take it indoors to help Santa, as he was always so busy on Christmas Eve, and now he wouldn't have to climb down Sam's chimney.

He could hardly wait to open it and look inside. Perhaps he would take a little peep, he thought.

He found his torch
and shone it inside.

A kite!
Santa had got his letter.
Sam tied the sack back up so Mum
and Dad wouldn't know he'd looked.

A large label hung from the end of the string.
"But wait a minute," thought Sam. "That's not my name!"
On the label, in neat black writing, it read
"Billy, love Santa x"
"Billy? Oh no, this isn't my sack,"
he cried.

Billy
love
Santa
x

Just at that moment, a lump of soot fell
down the chimney and Sam could hear
puffing and panting from above.

"It must be Santa," he thought.
"I'll have to hide this sack or
he'll take it away and I won't
get my kite." Sam pulled the
sack under the stairs and
closed the door.

When he was finally brave enough to open it, he could see another large sack beside the fireplace, soot prints on the floor and the mince pie, sherry and carrots had gone.

"Good!" thought Sam. "Now I'll have two sacks to open in the morning!" He was just about to tear the label off Billy's sack when he began to think about Billy.

Who was Billy?
Where did he live?
Sam thought about
Christmas morning at Billy's
house. What would happen
when he came downstairs
to find no sack of presents?

But Sam really wanted that kite. Sam thought about Billy again. Billy would be really sad. Billy would think Santa had forgotten him. But Santa never forgets anyone.

Sam quickly pulled the sack back out onto the lawn, just where it had landed. To help Santa find the sack, Sam pushed his torch into the top of the sack and shone it skywards. Then he turned out of the cold night air, back indoors.

He tiptoed upstairs and slipped under the warm bed covers. There he lay, hoping that Santa would find Billy's sack. Tired from his night of adventure, he quickly fell asleep.

He awoke early, as the sun
began to rise and shine
across his sleepy face.
He rushed to the window, and
to his horror, he could see his
Dad in the middle of the lawn.

"Hadn't Santa found Billy's sack? Had his Dad found it instead? What about Billy?" worried Sam.

Sam rushed downstairs.

"Happy Christmas!" shouted his Mum and Dad.

"Look, Santa's been," said Mum.

"Don't look so worried, he hasn't forgotten you!"

"I see you were out looking for him too," smiled Dad.

"You left your torch out there and I could see your footprints in the frost! You rascal," he giggled.

Sam sighed with relief and hurriedly
opened the top of his sack.
"A kite!" he shrieked.
Sam was delighted.
He checked the label on the sack
to make sure. Yes, it really
was his this time.

Sam got dressed as quickly as
he could and rushed outside
with his kite to the local park.

Lots of children were there with their new toys.
Sam could see a little boy flying a kite just like his.

"Hello," he said. "What's your name?"
"Billy," said the boy. "Billy!" gasped Sam.
"Yes, Billy!" he smiled.

Sam's face beamed as
he launched his kite
beside his new friend.